LINDA MILSTEIN

Miami-Nanny Stories

PICTURES BY OKI S. HAN

TAMBOURINE BOOKS / NEW YORK

FRANKLIN PIERCE COLLEGE
LIBRARY
RINDGE, NEW HAMPSHIRE

Text copyright © 1994 by Linda Breiner Milstein.   Illustrations copyright © 1994 by Oki S. Han.
All rights reserved.   No part of this book may be reproduced or utilized in any form or by any means,
electronic or mechanical, including photocopying, recording, or by any information storage or retrieval
system, without permission in writing from the Publisher.   Inquiries should be addressed to
Tambourine Books, a division of William Morrow & Company, Inc.,
1350 Avenue of the Americas, New York, New York 10019.
Printed in the United States of America.
The text type is Monotype Bell.

Library of Congress Cataloging in Publication Data
Milstein, Linda Breiner. Miami-Nanny stories/Linda Breiner Milstein; illustrated by Oki S. Han. — 1st ed. p. cm.
Summary: Three stories describe the special relationship between two children and their grandmother.
1. Children's stories, American. [1. Grandmothers—Fiction. 2. Jews—Fiction. 3. Family life—Fiction.]
I. Han, Oki S., ill. II. Title. PZ7.M6446Mi 1994 [E]—dc20 93-28680 CIP AC
ISBN 0-688-11151-3 (TR). — ISBN 0-688-11152-1 (LE)
1 3 5 7 9 10 8 6 4 2
First edition

CURR
PZ
7
.m6446
mi
1994

To my mother-in-law, Tanya Friedman (Miami-Nanny),
and my mother, Beatrice Breiner (Michigan-Nanny),
and all the wonderful nannies everywhere.   L.M.

For my mother.
Special thanks to all the friends who have been praying with
me for strength and peace from the Lord.   O.S.H.

Miami-Nanny

When Miami-Nanny came to visit, she always carried at least one shopping bag. She liked to say certain things have to travel that way.

When Miami-Nanny came to visit, Dad said, "Be good."

"Okay," said Sophie.

"No kisses," said Joey.

"Be good," said Dad.

When Miami-Nanny came to visit, Mom said, "Remember your manners."

"Okay," said Sophie.

"Just hugs," said Joey.

"Remember your manners," said Mom.

When Miami-Nanny came to visit, Joey and Sophie said, "I hope she brought toys."

"No matter what, say thank you," said Mom and Dad.

"Hi, Miami-Nanny!" everybody said.

"And what is this? Where are my hugs and kisses?" Miami-Nanny said. Then she grabbed Joey and Sophie with a bear hug and covered them with mushy kisses.

"I'm too big for kisses," said Joey.

"Not me!" said Sophie and gave Miami-Nanny her best hug.

Finally, Joey couldn't stand it any longer. "Did you bring me a toy?" he said.

Mom and Dad tried to give him the remember-your-manners look. But Miami-Nanny laughed and began unpacking the shopping bags.

First there was a gift box Miami-Nanny had saved. "You never know," she said, "a good box, a nice shopping bag, it might come in handy." She lifted the top off. "I thought maybe you could use a nice jacket or an extra shirt."

In no time everyone was wearing matching T-shirts and jackets.

"Just a little something, in case it gets cold," Miami-Nanny said. "By us it's so hot, but here, you never know."

"Thank you, Miami-Nanny," they said.

Next there was a shoe box. Inside of it were five layers of tightly packed, aluminum-foil-wrapped, chocolate-chip mandelbread, as usual.

"Thank you, Miami-Nanny," they said.

Miami-Nanny reached into the shopping bag and pulled out another box. "Here's something special I've been saving just for you, Joey. It was Papa's. Now it's yours," she said.

Joey slowly unwrapped the special something of Papa's, that Miami-Nanny had saved in its own box.

"It's Papa's radio car," said Mom. "You never used to let me go near it when I was Joey's age!"

"You live and learn," said Miami-Nanny. Then she showed Joey how the gearshift turned it on and off, and how the steering wheel changed the stations, and how the wheels really moved.

"Thanks Miami-Nanny! I like it!" said Joey, and waited until she wasn't looking before he wiped her kisses off.

Miami-Nanny dug deep into a shopping bag. She pulled out a lumpy package.

"Is that for me?" whispered Sophie.

"Let's find out," Miami-Nanny said.

Inside was a cloth doll with a hand-painted face. "She's beautiful," said Sophie and scooped her up. "And she's soft, like a pillow."

"That's because she's stuffed with feathers," Miami-Nanny said.

"It's a very special doll," whispered Mom, "and very old."

"It belonged to my little sister," said Miami-Nanny. "She gave it to me to remember her by, when I left home."

"Thank you," said Sophie. "She's the best doll in the world."

"We always thought so," Miami-Nanny said.

"And this is for you, dear," said Miami-Nanny. She handed Mom a box that had been wrapped so well, for so long, it took several minutes to open up.

"It's my old samovar! Tante Freida gave it to me when I was a little girl. I thought I ruined it. I thought you got rid of it years ago."

"It's a little scratched and dented, but so what. It cleaned up nice. And what a sight you were, lugging that samovar around the sandbox!"

Everybody laughed trying to imagine Mom as a little girl.

"And this is for you," Miami-Nanny said, as she handed Dad a flat box. Inside was a picture frame. "I decorated it myself."

"How nice, Ma. I don't think I ever saw this picture of Sophie before," said Dad.

"That's not Sophie," said Miami-Nanny. "That's Sophie's mom."

"Oooohh," said Sophie, trying hard to see.

Suddenly, Joey shouted, "The samovar!"

Everybody looked. It was the little samovar all right, and the baby in the picture sat clutching it close to herself.

In no time at all everyone was enjoying music from Papa's radio car, while they sipped fresh samovar tea and feasted on chocolate-chip mandelbread, straight from the shoe box.

"We're glad you're here, Ma," said Mom and Dad.

Sophie said, "Me, too."

"Catch!" called Joey and blew Miami-Nanny his best kiss.

"Such a family!" said Miami-Nanny as she looked around the table. And she was right.

"Such a Miami-Nanny!" said Mom and Dad and Joey and Sophie. And they were right too.

What Papa Joe Did

Joey had been visiting Miami-Nanny since the weekend.

"There's nothing to do here," said Joey.

"How about going swimming?" Miami-Nanny said.

"That's all I ever do," said Joey.

"Are you thirsty? Do you want to eat a little something?"

"I'm not hungry," said Joey.

"Should I tell you a story?"

"I'm too old for stories." Joey said.

"We could take a nice walk on the beach."

"Oh, okay," Joey mumbled. "But not a long one."

"Just long enough," Miami-Nanny said.

"Come, give a look," she said.

"Dolphins!" shouted Joey. "They're so fast!"

"It's just like watching Joe. May he rest in peace," Miami-Nanny said.

"Papa Joe?" he said.

"Who else? He'd swim right out there, whenever he had the chance."

"What's out there?" asked Joey.

"Just water and freedom," Miami-Nanny said.

"He must have been strong," said Joey.

"Like an ox! And fast!"

"How fast?" asked Joey.

"Fast enough to save his life. He used to swim straight out until he was a speck."

Joey whistled. "That's strong!"

"Strong arms and a strong head. But it's getting late. Let's go in."

"Wait. Tell me how swimming saved his life. Did he get lost?"

"It should only have been so simple," Miami-Nanny said. "No, this happened a long time ago."

"What happened?" asked Joey.

"There was a terrible war in the place we were born."

"I thought Papa Joe lived here," said Joey.

"Not until much later. During the war they made laws that stopped people from going where they wanted to go. He was stuck! And *that's* when the enemy captured him," said Miami-Nanny as her fingers went *snap!*

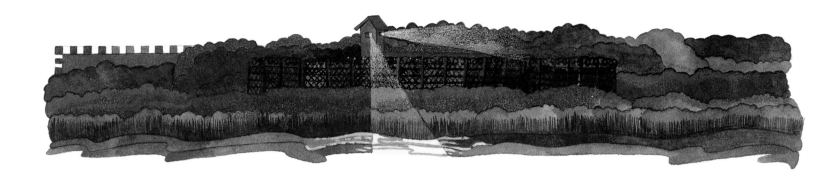

"Was he alone?" asked Joey. "Was he scared?"

"Sometimes he was scared. But he was never alone. He was with lots of people he knew."

"I wouldn't be scared," said Joey. And he threw a stone at the waves. "Was he in jail?"

"Not exactly," said Miami-Nanny. "Everyone that got caught was sent to a special prison in the middle of the woods."

"I would run the fastest and get out!" said Joey. And he raced ahead.

"People tried," said Miami-Nanny. "But there was a big fence all around."

"I would climb the highest fence and jump over the top!" said Joey. And he made his biggest leap.

"The fence was too high and too sharp. Besides, the guards were watching," Miami-Nanny said.

"I would go at night when no one could see," said Joey. And he pretended to sneak in the dark.

"There was a thick forest all around," said Miami-Nanny, "with a huge lake along one side."

"I'm not afraid of trees and animals!" said Joey. And he showed how he'd ambush his prey.

"That's what Papa Joe thought," Miami Nanny said.

"Did he climb over the fence at night? Did he camp out in the woods?"

"Close," she said. "One cloudy night he crept to the fence and crawled through a hole."

"Yes! I would find a hole," said Joey. And he belly crawled in the sand. "Then did he run fast?"

"No," whispered Miami-Nanny. "He slipped into the lake and started to swim."

"Was the lake big?" asked Joey.

"Bigger than a hundred pools. He swam and swam, faster than the guards could run or shoot!"

"Wow!" said Joey. "He swam far!"

"For three hours he swam. Finally he made it to the other side."

"And then he came here?" asked Joey.

"First he found some of his friends and together they fought back until everyone was free."

"Hurrah! Hurrah!" cheered Joey. And he jumped up and down with each shout.

"Now, you must be hungry after such a long walk."

"And thirsty," Joey said.

"Yes," laughed Miami-Nanny, "after so much talk."

So Miami-Nanny and Joey sat down and drank seltzer and fresh-squeezed orange juice and munched on garlic pickles and talked.

"You know, you're named after him," said Miami-Nanny. "Such a fine boy. Joe would have been proud."

"Can I go swimming tomorrow?" asked Joey.

"I thought you were in such a hurry to go home?"

"I don't want to go yet. I need to practice my swimming first," he said.

"If you don't want to, then you don't need to," Miami-Nanny agreed.

"I like it here," said Joey.

"So next time stay longer," said Miami-Nanny and gave Joey a real Nanny kiss.

Itza-Není

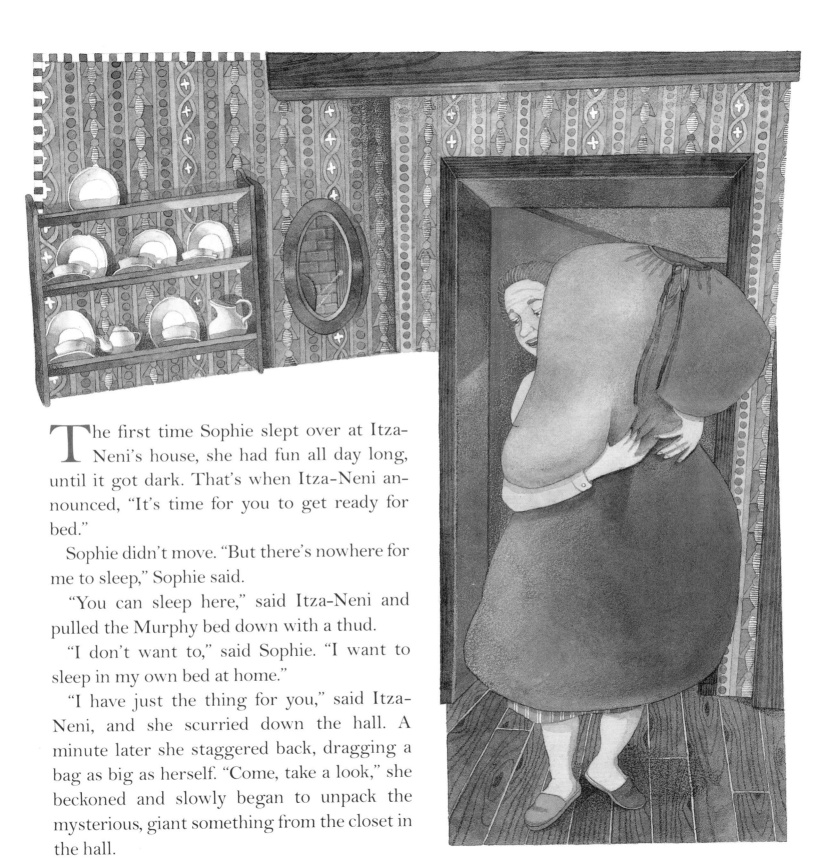

The first time Sophie slept over at Itza-Neni's house, she had fun all day long, until it got dark. That's when Itza-Neni announced, "It's time for you to get ready for bed."

Sophie didn't move. "But there's nowhere for me to sleep," Sophie said.

"You can sleep here," said Itza-Neni and pulled the Murphy bed down with a thud.

"I don't want to," said Sophie. "I want to sleep in my own bed at home."

"I have just the thing for you," said Itza-Neni, and she scurried down the hall. A minute later she staggered back, dragging a bag as big as herself. "Come, take a look," she beckoned and slowly began to unpack the mysterious, giant something from the closet in the hall.

At first glance it was a pillow, large and fat. But it didn't end when Sophie lifted a corner out. The more they pulled, the more it emerged until the whole Murphy bed was swamped. They shook it and shook it and fluffed it up two feet thick. "This, Sophie, is a real feather bed," Itza-Neni announced. Sophie leapt into the middle. It was like falling into a cloud. "I never saw this before," said Sophie.

"It was a gift a long time ago, from a girl named Bella, in the old country," Itza-Neni began. "She came from a poor family. The papa worked hard, but still, they barely had enough to make ends meet."

"Did her mama work?"

"Oh, yes! But," whispered Itza-Neni, "she needed Bella's help."

"Why?" asked Sophie.

"Back then, all the mamas made everything by hand, from scratch."

"Did Bella help after school?" asked Sophie.

"There was no school for Bella."

"Why not?"

"In those days girls didn't always go to school, especially with five brothers and a baby sister in the house."

"That was no fair for Bella."

"No, but that's how life is sometimes. You just have to keep trying, no matter what. The older boys studied, so someone had to stay behind to help."

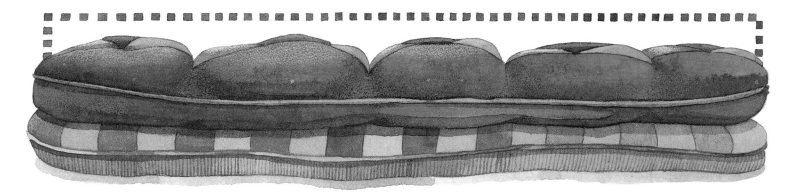

"Maybe if Bella hurried home from school real fast, then she could help her mama in the afternoon, after school?"

"There was a lot to do. You tell me what you think. First there was the cooking," said Itza-Neni counting on one hand. "And there was the cleaning, the shopping, the feeding," she said, tapping a finger for each. "Next there was the carrying, the mending, the fixing, the washing, the pressing, the knitting, the sewing, the pickling, the kneading, the baking, and doctoring for the house. Then there was feeding the chickens and collecting and sorting and selling their eggs. And then there was tending the geese."

"I guess she was too busy for school," Sophie said.

"And when she was done with her chores," said Itza-Neni, "she'd prepare goose feathers, like these. Bella made this feather bed. She made lots of beds like these."

"Why?" Sophie asked.

"Some were for the family to use and some were to sell. Everyone in the town wanted one of Bella's extra fluffy feather beds. She was always busy sorting feathers, even when she baby-sat. She used to let her baby sister chase the downy fuzz. She was very clever, Bella was, about things like that."

"I wish I could make a feather bed," Sophie said.

"There were things Bella wished she could do, too, like read," said Itza-Neni.

"She couldn't read?"

"How could she? She never went to school. And she was busy with babies or chores or chickens or feathers from morning till night."

"I go to school. Next year I'm going to do homework like Joey, every day."

"I'm glad," said Itza-Neni. "Unfortunately, no one thought Bella should learn. Everyone already depended on her for so much else."

"What did she do?" asked Sophie.

"She helped the mama. She thought and dreamed and sometimes she was sad. Then one year, the same year she made this very feather bed, Bella got very sick and had to rest a long, long time."

"Was she okay?" asked Sophie.

"In the end she was just fine. But while she was sick the mama couldn't keep up with all the housework herself."

"What happened?" asked Sophie.

"When the entire household became a mess, the rest of the family started to help the mama with the chores. And while Bella was recovering all those weeks and weeks in bed, she finally had the time to learn to read. Before she was well, she had read half the books in the house."

"What happened then?" asked Sophie.

"Bella's parents understood they had been wrong."

"And unfair," said Sophie.

"So from that day, she was allowed to go to school. That's why Bella never made another feather bed. This one was the very last."

"I love this feather bed," said Sophie snuggling into its warmth. "But what happened to Bella?"

"She finished school, grew up, and came here to live. Bella gave me this feather bed just before she left. Later, I brought it with me. And now, I want to give it to you."

"Oh, thank you Itza-Neni! Thank you! But what happened to her?" Sophie asked.

"She worked at this and that, got married, had children, and now grandchildren too. They call her Nanny."

"You mean, she's my Miami-Nanny?"

"That's right," said Itza-Neni. "And guess who her baby sister is."

"You?" asked Sophie.

"How did you know?" said Itza-Neni and smiled. "Now, bedtime for you."

They shook the old feather bed one corner at a time. It was much too heavy to lift and shake the whole thing all at once. Sophie leapt into the middle.

"Good night," said Itza-Neni and kissed her grandniece on both cheeks. "Sweet dreams Mama-lah."

"Sweet dreams," Sophie said.

FRANKLIN PIERCE COLLEGE LIBRARY

00081994

DATE DUE

MAR 0 7 1995			
JUL 1 1995			
JAN 2 8 98			
MAY 0 4 03			
JUL 1 1 2011			
GAYLORD			PRINTED IN U.S.A.